Happy Birdday, Tacky!

Written by Helen Lester
Illustrated by Lynn Munsinger

Houghton Mifflin Books for Children
Houghton Mifflin Harcourt
BOSTON NEW YORK 2013

To all those who can't wait for their next birdday—from one who can!
—H.L.

Text copyright © 2013 by Helen Lester
Illustrations copyright © 2013 by Lynn Munsinger

Houghton Mifflin Books for Children is an imprint of
Houghton Mifflin Harcourt Publishing Company.

www.hmhbooks.com

The text of this book is set in Garamond.

Library of Congress Cataloging-in-Publication Data
Lester, Helen.
Happy birdday, Tacky! / written by Helen Lester and illustrated by Lynn Munsinger.
p. cm.
Summary: Goodly, Lovely, Angel, Neatly, and Perfect have spent weeks planning the
perfect party to celebrate Tacky's hatchday, and while nothing turns out quite
as they expected, the penguins and their special guest have a wonderful time.
ISBN 978-0-547-91228-8
[1. Birthdays—Fiction. 2. Parties—Fiction. 3. Dance—Fiction. 4. Penguins—Fiction.]
I. Munsinger, Lynn, ill. II. Title. III. Title: Happy birthday, Tacky!
PZ7.L56285Hap 2013
[E]—dc23
2012014847

Manufactured in China
SCP 10 9 8 7 6 5 4 3 2 1
4500394671

The Nice Icy Land was crackling with busy-ness.

For weeks Goodly, Lovely, Angel, Neatly, and Perfect had been planning a Perfect Party for Tacky the Penguin's Birdday. There was a whole lot of baking and wrapping and whispering going on.

Of course they made birdday cards, but since Tacky was an odd bird with an odd way of counting, it only made sense that he had told them odd things about how old he was.

The day before the Perfect Party, the penguins went through their plan book.

Cards? Check.

Song? Check.

Present? Check.

Fishy ice cream? Check.

Cake? Check.

Surprise entertainment? Check.

"Everything's perfect!" declared Perfect.
(This confused his companions, for as far as they knew, *Perfect* was Perfect. But never mind.)

They were ready to surprise Tacky with a Perfect Birdday Party.

So the next morning, "Oh, Taaaaaacky!" they called.
Tacky didn't seem to hear them. He had invented a wonderful
Flapwaddle Dance and was quite busy flippiting about in his
own little world.

Three steps left

and three steps right

Do it on your tippywebs to get some height

Flap your flippers like you're gonna take flight
Stomp three times and say, "ALL RIGHT!"

Three steps left and—

"TAAACCCKKKKYYYY!"

Tacky paused in mid-flapwaddle. "What's happening?"
"SURPRISE!" the penguins chorused. "Happy birdday!"

"For ME?" Tacky was thrilled as he beheld the beautiful cards they offered him. And more thrilled when they burst into the birdday song.

Happy birdday to you
Happy birdday to you
It's your own special hatchday
Happy birdday to you!

Then they led him to the present.
"Wow!" blared Tacky. "What is it?"
"It's a . . . er . . . dinner jacket."

"Dinner jacket? Should I eat it?"
"Not at the moment," they gulped.

"Well, thank you. Hey, ribbons for everyone!"

Hmm. Is this penguin decoration in our Perfect Party plan book? the companions wondered as they stumbled on to the refreshment table. But they were too polite to ask.

"Way cool!" exclaimed Tacky. He took a cone, filled it with
fishy ice cream, and plopped it down on his head. "Looky!
A birdday hat!"
"A birdday hat," echoed his companions,
thinking, *Definitely NOT in our Perfect Party plan book.*

But there, there, they must get on with the festivities. Out came the cake.

When the candles had been blown out, Goodly asked, "Tacky, will you please pass the cake?"

"You betcha!" chirped Tacky. He did a nifty forward pass to Perfect,

who lateraled to Lovely,

who flipped the cake to Angel,

who spiraled to Neatly, who tossed it to Goodly,

who wasn't very
athletic and dropped it.
Oops.

As they nibbled the smushy cake, the companions wondered,
*How **IM**PERFECT can a Perfect Party get????????*
They were soon to find out.

It was time for the perfect ending. The surprise entertainment.
This was going to be the crown jewel of their party. Absolutely.
Goodly, Lovely, Angel, Neatly, and Perfect had outdone
themselves, for they had brought in Twinklewebs the Dance
Queen, all the way from Iglooslavia.

And there she was! WOW!

Twinklewebs announced,
"I vant to perform for you a denz peez from *Swan Frozen-Body-of-Water.*"

Gracefully she floated this way, that way, and the other way, charming her audience. This way, that way, the other way, and then the **wrong way.**

"Gasp!" gasped Goodly, Lovely, Angel, Neatly, and Perfect.
"Nice landing!" exclaimed Tacky.

And Twinklewebs, who was not only the Dance Queen but a first-rate drama queen, wailed, "Mine webby! Mine beaudyful left webby is eenjured. I shall never denz again. Mine career is kaputted. I shall die right here. Like now."
Twinklewebs closed her eyes.

How imperfect.

Goodly looked at Lovely, who looked at Angel, who looked at
Neatly, who looked at Perfect, who looked back at Goodly.
Oh, deary. What to do now?

They hovered over Twinklewebs, wringing their flippers
and becoming covered with perspiration icicles.
What a dreadful end for their Perfect Party.
They were ready to tear their hair, if only they had any.

Meanwhile, Tacky, who had been distracted by some cake crumbs on his foot and thus did not realize the seriousness of the situation, hopped up on the stage. "Hey, want to see a crummy dance? Get it? Crumbs? *Crummy?* Hee hee."

And with that he began his Flapwaddle Dance.

Three steps left and three steps right

Twinklewebs opened one eye.

Do it on your tippywebs to get some height

Twinklewebs opened the other eye.

Flap your flippers like you're gonna take flight

Now Twinklewebs was up on her feet.

Stomp three times and say, "ALL RIGHT!"

"ALL RIGHT!" exclaimed Twinklewebs,
whose beautiful left webby suddenly felt much better. She
hopped back on the stage.

"Thet denz. Thet beaudyful denz peez. I vant it. I must hev it.

Show me."

She followed Tacky step for step, and by the third time, Tacky's five party penguins had recovered and hopped to the stage.

Now everybody joined in!

Three steps left and three steps right
Do it on your tippywebs to get some height

Flap your flippers like you're gonna take flight
Stomp three times and say, "ALL RIGHT!"

Hooray! It *was* the Perfect Party after all.
Twinklewebs gave Tacky an autograph. And a beeg keess.
Then everybody hugged Tacky.
Tacky was an odd bird, but a nice bird to have around.
And a perfect bird to have at a party!